W9-BUX-817

archyology ii

archyology ii
(the final dig)

---

the long lost tales of archy and mehitabel

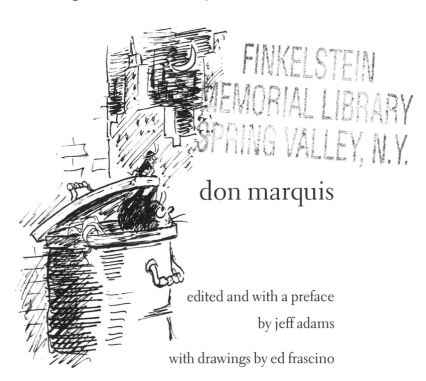

FINKELSTEIN
MEMORIAL LIBRARY
SPRING VALLEY, N.Y.

don marquis

edited and with a preface
by jeff adams

with drawings by ed frascino

university press of new england
hanover and london

FINKELSTEIN MEMORIAL LIBRARY

3 2191 00544 1349

for jane pepe

university press of new england

hanover, nh 03755

this compilation © 1998 by jeff adams

illustrations © 1998 by ed frascino

all rights reserved

printed in the united states of america

5 4 3 2 1

cip data appear at the end of the book

designed by mike burton

contents

v

preface

This is the second and final volume presenting the long lost tales of Archy the Cockroach and Mehitabel the Alley Cat, two characters immortalized by Don Marquis, who was one of the most popular American humorists of the early twentieth century. The tales were discovered, quite by accident, in a steamer trunk stored in a Brooklyn warehouse, where they had languished undisturbed among the author's papers since his death in 1937. The inimitable Archy stories appeared in Marquis's newspaper columns and other publications from 1916 through the 1930s. Now, after more than 60 years in that trunk, Archy returns with all new delights for a whole new generation of readers.

Don Marquis earned his living chiefly as a newspaper columnist, for many years writing for the *New York Sun* and later for the *Herald Tribune*. While he was successful in this line of work, higher literary aspirations propelled him to compose short stories, novels, serious poetry, and plays, always with the thought that he would someday achieve recognition as a serious writer. In a 1928 essay for *The Saturday Evening Post* he wrote, "I got to seeing that column as a grave, twenty-three inches long, into which I buried a part of myself every day—a part that I tore, raw and bleeding, from my brain."

For Marquis, life as a newspaperman became a constant search for material to fill his column, especially the kind that would keep it lively. He wrote, "Besides the verse, paragraphs, sketches, fables and occasional serious expressions of opinion, I began to create characters through whom I might comment upon or satirize current phases of existence, or whom I might develop for the sheer pleasure of creation."

A number of these characters became quite popular, but none equaled the popularity of Archy, the cockroach who claimed to possess the transmigrated soul of a dead poet. Archy's first appearance heralded the arrival of a bug whose need for expression was all-consuming. So strong was his drive to create, the story went, that he would climb up on the keys of Marquis's typewriter and hurl himself downward, headfirst, to punch out his message by hitting one key at a time—a process that would produce only one painful letter per leap. Since he couldn't simultaneously operate the shift key, Archy's missives appeared in lower case. Archy often referred to Marquis as his "boss," and fully expected to see his hard-won writings appear prominently in the daily column.

In one brilliant stroke, Archy's travail became the metaphor for Marquis's own literary struggle. But in another sense Archy was Marquis's alter ego and gave the author a charming platform from which to comment on virtually any topic, from the lighthearted to the serious, for the entertainment—and edification—of his readers. Archy's most frequent companion was Mehitabel the Alley Cat, who claimed to have once been Cleopatra and whose lust for life inspired her motto "toujours gai."

The irony of Archy's popularity didn't escape Marquis in his lifetime, and even today the enchanting relevance of these lost tales speaks to the character's continuing appeal. I can tell you that the reason for this is simple: the stuff is so much fun to read that it brings a smile to your face.

Of course you may find yourself going back to the stories, inspired or provoked by something that caught your attention, and find even more to like. And after all, isn't that the mark of a great writer? Enjoy.

JEFF ADAMS

archyology ii

consider

every time
i get to feeling
bad because
i am a cockroach
i think how
much worse it would be
if i were a
seventeen year
locust and only woke
up once every
seventeen years
yours for the second
coming of bacchus

archy

the inventor s toothpick

boss mehitabel the cat was in here
last evening and said archy what are
you going to give up for the duration of
    the
war i can t give up food i
told her the boss has quit feeding me
almost entirely what are you going to
    give
up mehitabel said she was going to
give up ratting the nerve of it boss it
has been six months since that
    lazy feline has
connected with a rodent i had quite an
adventure the other evening i dropped
    into a
pitcher of ale in an up town place
for a swim and a nightcap and the
    fellow that
fished me out was an inventor i have
    here he said
taking out an old fashioned snuff box an
explosive so high that one grain of it
    would blow
hoboken into an american city be
gentle with it said his vis a vis never
    fear
said the inventor it is trained it only
    bites when
i sick it onto something it has to be
    rubbed

2

against another chemical to detonate and
here is the other chemical he fished out
    a little bit of
each on the end of a quill tooth pick
    there is
enough here he said to
blow the curse out of potsdam his vis a
    vis
turned pale gulped and began to choke
    i have

partly swallowed my teeth he said in a
guttural tone they are half
way down but don t bother to slap me
on the
back you might hit me with the wrong
hand as he spoke
he coughed and the wind of the
cough blew the high explosive off the
end
of the inventor s tooth pick it
fell onto my damp back as gently as a
snow flake and
on account of the dampness it stuck
there i
don t know whether he ever recovered
his teeth or
not for i ran away from there in a panic
squirming as i ran and expecting
the explosion any instant the two power
ful
chemicals lay side by side on my back
a touch would
mix them and they would detonate and
manhattan
island would be but a memory but
after i
had run for a while i began to get
calmer for i realized that i could not run
away from what was on my back a
strange sense of exhilaration succeeded
my
fear i felt that i was the most
destructive thing in the universe
ha ha i cried to the crowds as i walked
boldly

down broadway and into columbus circle
many a time i have dodged your
    feet but
step on me now if you dare and i
walked boldly past the hatboy and into
    a gilded

resort of what mehitabel calls the
jewness doughray the hat check boy
    stamped
at me and i never dodged as well now
    as any
time i said and laughed to think the
fate of six million people was on a
cockroach s back the foot descended and
    as fate
would have it the instep of the hat check
    boy

arched over me his heel or his
toe would have crushed me and he would
      have
received the biggest tip on record ha ha i
said you that have scorned the
humble cockroach are now in his power
      and
walked across the dancing floor too
      proud to
dodge a foot but luck was with new
york once again one young man was
      about to
step on me when his fair partner cried
      no do
not kill him it may be archy that
word of humanity saved the town it
aroused my better nature i abandoned
      my
idea of getting stepped on and
went and dried my back at an electric
      fan which
would allow the powerful chemicals to
      slip off when i
shrugged my shoulders then carefully
      balancing
myself so my shoulders would not shrug
      too
soon i traversed the town once
more with my terrible burden and
finally deposited it in
a german bar room where i have every
reason to believe that treason is being
      plotted i
took it into the center of a swiss cheese
and carefully shrugged it off my back
investigations lead me to believe that
      there

is a plot to smuggle that cheese into
germany through holland for
the kaiser s own table i hope the crown
prince is present when wilhelm bites it

archy

open spaces

i was talking with an old
spider in your
office the other day
human beings
said she grow crueller
and crueller
as the years go by
little they care if their
fellow creatures perish
of starvation
what with all these
screens to keep flies
out of houses
and all this sticky flypaper
to catch them when
they get in a spider
can scarcely pick up
an honest living any more
but man in his selfishness
cares nothing for that
i am tired of houses
i am going to find a park
to live in i am
going out into the great
open spaces where insects
are insects
did it ever occur
to you i asked her
that men probably think
it will make very little

difference to their universe
if all the spiders in it
cease to exist
how strange she replied
i have had the very
same thought with regard
to human beings

archy

The

Great False Teeth

Mystery

A Sequel to The Great Goulash Mystery

CHAPTER ONE

The following advertisement appeared in a New York newspaper on Monday, September 8, 1919:

LOST—VERY LIBERAL REWARD for the return of removable gold and platinum bridgework upper and lower TEETH, lost in Hotel Martinique on Friday night or early Saturday morning; return of above appreciated and no questions asked. J. J. McLaughlin, Hotel Martinique, 32nd Street and Broadway.

CHAPTER TWO

It was night.

But it was not so dark that an observer sitting on one of the benches of the City Hall Park might not have seen two airplanes rapidly circling around the tower of the Woolworth Building five or six hundred feet above the street level.

Put-put-put! went the motors.

One of them was pursuing the other one.

Round and round they went.

They passed so close to the tower that at times their wings scraped the architecture.

Sometimes the one which was being pursued would gain a little, which would bring it into the rear of the one that was doing the pursuing, and this would make it appear that the one which was really doing the pursuing was the one which was being pursued.

And then the one which was doing the pursuing would also sprint for a few seconds and make up the distance which it had lost.

Both were handled by expert aviators.

Neither showed any lights. All was darkness except for the sparks which would appear when the architecture was scraped.

These sparks made a ring of fire around the building.

Put-put-put! went the motors.

Suddenly another noise resounded.

Rat-tat-tat! mingled with the put-put-put!

They were shooting at each other with machine guns.

The glare of the machine guns was now added to the ring of sparks that resulted when the tips of the wings would strike the architecture.

Rat-tat-tat! went the guns. One would have thought they were riveting something.

CHAPTER THREE

At the foot of the Woolworth Building stood a gigantic cockroach.

He looked upward, balancing himself on the curbstone.

What could he be doing here? And why?

It was Archy, the Cockroach Detective.

CHAPTER FOUR

A moth fluttered down.

It fell at the Cockroach Detective's feet.

It had seen the glare of fire circling the Woolworth Tower and had flown into it.

Archy examined it.

"It has been killed by a machine gun bullet," the Cockroach Detective murmured, "of the regulation army caliber."

A mystery was going on above.

CHAPTER FIVE

Suddenly one of the airplanes crashed into the other one. Both were wrecked.

Neither aviator had time to unfurl his parachute.

Both machines caught fire in the air.

Down, down, down fell the flaming machines!

They struck the pavement in a little heap of ashes which were blown hither and thither.

Only one thing remained unburned.

That was a set of false teeth.

They were richly wrought by some master dentist.

Gold, ivory and platinum entered into their architecture.

They were the teeth of a millionaire. Archy could see that at a glance.

No poor person could have afforded them.

No one in even moderate circumstances could have bought the kind of food that would naturally go with them.

Such was the Cockroach Detective's first thought.

CHAPTER SIX

A costly jewel here and there was scattered amongst them.

They were teeth that might have graced the boudoir table of a duchess of the old regime.

Archy, with his microscopic eye, saw something clinging to one of the jewels.

He uttered an exclamation.

Hastily producing from his knapsack a slab of some strange looking substance he fitted the teeth into dents that had been made in it before it hardened.

The teeth exactly fit the dents.

"Ha! Ha!" cried Archy, the Cockroach Detective, "I

thought so! These teeth fit the goulash! They fit the goulash!"

CHAPTER SEVEN

The Detective was hastening toward the entrance to the Seventh Avenue Subway with both teeth and goulash in his possession when a five-ton motor truck was deliberately driven at him.

The wheels passed over the Detective.

He loosed the teeth and goulash from his grasp.

A beautiful woman sprang from the seat beside the driver, picked up the teeth and goulash and ordered the driver to proceed toward the Staten Island Ferry.

She had raven hair.

A glance would have been enough to place her as one who probably had in times past been willing to go to almost any lengths to satisfy the cravings of a predominant will power which showed itself in her firm chin and the decided way in which she climbed back onto the truck again and ordered the chauffeur to break all the speed laws, as she had influence enough with the authorities to see that he was not fined if he did so.

She had an air of command.

CHAPTER EIGHT

But was Archy dead?

Not he!

The truck had a dent in the wheel which ran over him and he nestled into the dent, so that the full force of the collision had not had its effect upon his being.

He was shaken and bruised and somewhat stunned. Gathering himself together he examined the fingerprints

in the dust that the raven haired woman had made when she hastily picked up the teeth.

In an instant he was off in pursuit.

(To be continued.)

a letter from mehitabel

well archy mehitabel says to
me as i cannot
work the typewriter would
you mind writing an open
letter for me
here goes i
said as she dictated
as follows to
the city government i
hear you are thinking
of employing a lot of
cats at six dollars and a
half a year
to keep the rats and mice
from eating the archives and
the tired employees
in the city offices i
can understand that
when an employee goes to sleep
he might be in great
danger of being eaten
what you want is cats with
some class to them
and you will not be able to
get them for the money
i have a large feline
acquaintance one or
two of them are cats
almost as big as a tiger
no reflection on tammany

is intended i could
get you the services of hundreds
of cats at a decent wage
but first it would take a
little propaganda to get the
right sort of cats
interested in the idea a
fund is necessary for the
propaganda i would be
willing to administer this
fund and get recruits and

organize them
for a good salary but lay off
the six dollar and a
half a year stuff

communicate any offer you have
to make through archy
my publicity agent and general
business representative

        mehitabel the cat
           per archy

dictated but not read
p s tell the
mayor if the price is
right i can get a cat
for the reporters room
at the city hall who
would be able to eat a
reporter in four or five
bites and who would be
willing to do so if
properly approached all
the mayor would need to do
would be to point out
which reporter and
this cat would do the
rest or we might agree on
a flat rate for all the
reporters or we could say
ten reporters a year for
ten dollars a reporter just
as soon as one reporter is
eaten another one will of course
take his place they
are fearless creatures these
reporters always willing
to go to their death
without stopping to make a
will but for a thousand
dollars a year i will agree to

keep the city hall
clear of reporters for at least
three days a week but
the first thing is the
propaganda fund

                    mehitabel
                        purr archy

Archy, our cockroach in whose body has migrated the soul of a poet, is thoroughly in sympathy with the efforts of the Simplified Spelling Board. As he has to jump on the keys of the typewriter headfirst every time he makes a letter, the fewer the letters the less toil for Archy. He tells us he was a rhymester too before he took to vers libre; and we find on our machine today the following expression of his sentiments.

Don Marquis

archy comes out for simplified spelling

the simplified speling bords stand
　　4 the shorter and uglier word
they want the old fashund stuf cand
　　joshbilingsgate stuf is preferd

and i in the noshun rejoic
　　it shud hav bin dun long b4
4 my ego in finding a voic
　　is making my cranium sor

i find it a heluva strain
　　2 butt in2 yor colum by hek
and i think in the end that my brain
　　wil telescope in2 my nek

in the small of my bak theres a kink
　　and the rapid sukseshin of shocks
is puting my chin on the blink

and merging my nees with my hocks

but the thing that most hurts me i
  swear
  is more than a fizical wo
tis the fact that the forid i wear
  is becuming uncomonly lo

i wunc had a brow that was hi
  with the thots in it lofty and wide
but now it sags over my eye
  and theres nothing important in
    side

heres luk 2 the simplified bord
  may they finish the work theyv be
    gun
my hart with thare harts in akord
  my mind and thare minds r as 1

                              archy

archy s own short course on entomology

yon wood louse is xylophagous
you d think his little tummy
and also his esophagus
would be dry as the sarcophagus
that holds an arid mummy

the tarantula is a spider
she lives on chives and chicory
she is adept at kickery
as ever was a terpsichore
and the devil is inside her

archy

The
Great False Teeth
Mystery

A Sequel to The Great Goulash Mystery

The Rajah of Pootrajambra, one of the most potential of Indian potentates, has among his jewels and treasures a set of wonderful teeth that are said to be at least four thousand years old. They are richly set in gold, platinum and gems. Two of the teeth are said to have belonged to Buddha himself and the other thirty were the property of great religious prophets; one belonged to Confucius and seven of them had been the property of Grand Lamas of Tibet.

Although the Rajah of Pootrajambra is entirely bald inside his mouth, as to both upper and lower jaws, he has never dared to wear these teeth. He does not feel that he is worthy of them. But a musical comedy troupe is stranded in Pootrajambra and the Rajah marries the twenty-four chorus girls, with one of whom he is desperately in love. He marries all of them in order that the one whom he really prefers may not become lonely in Pootrajambra, and because he feels that the forty Oriental wives that he already has will not be able in their jealousy to persecute twenty-four Occidental wives as successfully as one. The one whom he really loves, whose name is Tessie De Montmorency, is perhaps the least worthy of his affections. She insists that he dine with her alone, on her birthday, which in itself scandalizes all his other wives, and that at this little tete-a-tete dinner he shall wear the sacred teeth. He protests. She says that if he does not do this she will understand that he does not love her. He is so infatuated that he can refuse her nothing, and finally yields.

Tessie introduces knockout drops into the Rajah's wine, and when he becomes unconscious she steals from his mouth the sacred teeth, substituting in their place a set of paste teeth which resemble them so that her crime will not be immediately discovered. She leaves Pootrajambra with the teeth, and a year later appears in London, where she becomes the bride of the Duke of Bilkington, one of the

proudest peers of England. The Duke adds the teeth to his famous collection at Bilkington House.

But Tessie is not very happy socially. A number of other former chorus girls, who have wedded English earls and dukes years before, make her feel that she is a newcomer. She and the Duke decide that it will be good policy to present the teeth to the Prime Minister, and he promises to use his influence to see that the duchesses and countesses of the older theatrical creations, several of whom have entered the aristocracy by way of the legitimate stage, keep their mouths shut and give Tessie a square deal.

The Premier's purpose is to present the teeth to one of the leaders of the Labor Party, whose support he needs in his Government and who dares not accept a peerage because of what the Cornish tin miners might think. The teeth he could accept without any apparent desertion of the cause of the laboring classes.

Tessie and the Duke put the teeth into a despatch box, ring for a messenger boy and start the teeth and the boy toward Downing Street. But on the way to Downing Street the boy goes into a movie theater, and on the screen he sees a drama which gives his innocent mind a bias toward crime. He determines to steal whatever may be in the despatch box, and, leaving the theater, goes down into the Whitechapel district to find a professional criminal who will give him advice as to just how to go about it. He is knocked on the head and the teeth are taken from him. He confesses, but the teeth are gone.

Scotland Yard is at once consulted by the Duke and the Prime Minister, and it is the opinion of Scotland Yard that the teeth are already on their way back to America. Inspector Dullish at once starts for America in a hydroplane. He arrives in time to take the teeth from the person of an international crook as the crook leaves an incoming vessel. Inspector Dullish is abducted that night, however, and wakes up the next day, without the teeth, in an abandoned barroom near the Great South Bay.

CHAPTER TEN

"Whatever shall I do now?" murmured Inspector Dullish.

There was no answer, in words. But a gigantic cockroach

on the abandoned bar seemed to be making signs to the Inspector.

"My word!" said the Inspector.

The cockroach dipped his legs into some of last year's beer which remained on the bar, and twisting his body about, and crawling back and forth, began to make letters in the counter.

"My eye!" said the Inspector. "Are you Harchy?"

The cockroach nodded.

"We have 'eard of you at 'ome," said the Inspector, doffing his hat respectfully. He read what Archy had written, and hope returned to him.

But just at that instant a Hindu person in the dress of a Swami rose up from behind the bar, smeared the writing with his sleeve, and shot the Inspector in the head.

The bullet ricocheted from the Inspector's skull and darted venomously toward the cockroach, who stood unflinching in its path.

"Aha!" cried the Hindu, perceiving Archy's danger.

Archy stood unmoved.

(To be continued.)

archy visits washington

washington d c july
23 well boss here
i am in washington
watching my step for fear
some one will push me
into the food bill up
to date i am the only thing
in the country that
has not been added to it by
the time this is
published nothing that
i have said may be
true however which is a
thing that is constantly happening
to thousands of
great journalists now in
washington it is so hot here that
i get stuck in the asphalt
every day on my
way from the senate press
gallery back to
shoemakers where the
affairs of the nation
are habitually settled by
the old settlers it
is so hot that you can
fry fish on the
sidewalk in any part of
town and many people
are here with fish to fry

including now
and then a german
carp i am lodging on
top of the washington
monument where i can
overlook things
you can t keep a good bug
from the top of
the column all the time i
am taking my meals with
the specimens in the
smithsonian institution when i
see any one coming i hold
my breath and look like another
specimen but in the
capitol building there
is no attention paid to me
because there are so
many other insects
around it gives you a
great idea of the
american people when you
see some of the
things they elect after july
27 address me care
st elizabeth hospital
for the insane i am going out
there for a visit with
some of your other
contributors

                                    archy

archy the insider

washington august 2 well
boss by the time you get this
something may be done
about cutting down the booze of
those fellows who are always coming into
your office and trying to
get you to go over to
liptons and have just one i am glad
to say that you always
resisted the temptation to go over
and have just one it looks to me
as if the bone dry idea
would triumph here there are so many
bones in the house and senate but
any news i send you will likely be un
    true by
the time you get it the more
important matter is the fact

that the official determination to
keep me an outsider here is
beginning to break down just a little bit
under my persistence i went
golfing with a high official yesterday he
was surprised when he opened his
bag and found me perched on a niblick
    you
see i am beginning to pick up some val
    uable
acquaintances and they all help my
one desire is to make myself useful to
the nation while i am in
washington also i was at dinner
yesterday with the second cousin
of the fourth assistant
doorkeeper of one of the committee
    rooms at
the capitol although it astonished him
    when
he saw me in the goulash but
you see that i am beginning to
break in i think you
had better keep me here as long as you
can stand the expense account i
was sworn at by a person
whom i afterward ascertained to be a
high official but am not at
liberty to reveal his name and position
    you
see i am coming on rapidly

                                    archy

all for brevier

thank you boss
for putting me in minion
type yesterday my hope is
that some day you will
print me in brevier as a regular
thing i hope i am not too
vain or egotistical but would love to
see myself in big type boss
i would do so much better work if you
gave me a chance to get
known a little better and make more
of a splurge yours for conspicuosity

archy

archyology

i see that these
excavators in egypt
have dug up
some canned beef 3350 years
old and they are
claiming it is the oldest
in the world but i
have some inside information
from some of my
colleagues who were
with the colors here
and there during the franker
part of the latest
war
and if my friends are to be
believed this canned
willie that king
tutankhamen s admirers
provided for him in his
tomb would be
considered a great delicacy
by the mess sergeants
in our army i
want to tell you it
takes courage
for the brave cockroaches
to follow the
flag but you will
notice they always
do

        archy

The
Great False Teeth
Mystery
or
All For Love's Sake

A Sequel to The Great Goulash Mystery

Henry Cleaver, a retired dollar a year man, gets into a taxi cab at the Union Station in Washington at 8:45 o'clock on Saturday evening, September 7, 1919, tells the chauffeur to drive him to the Willard Hotel and lights one of his favorite cigars, a Doloroso Enduro. At 8:52 he alights and is about to pay the driver when he suddenly exclaims: "But this is not the Willard!" "No sir," says the chauffeur, "this is the Biltmore." "But is there a Biltmore in Washington?" asks Cleaver. "I don't know anything about Washington," says the driver, "but there's a Biltmore in New York, and this is it." And the taxi man drives away.

Cleaver rejects the conclusion that he has traveled from Washington to New York by taxi cab in seven minutes; and yet he cannot understand what has happened. Between his teeth is the same Doloroso Enduro cigar that he lighted when he got into the taxi cab.

He takes it from his mouth and as he does so all his teeth fall out into his hand. He looks at these teeth in growing wonder. He has never known before that he has false teeth. And these false teeth are wonderful things in themselves; they are made of gold and platinum and ivory, with rich jewels set among them here and there. He walks into the lobby with the teeth in his hands and is immediately arrested by the house detective in spite of the protests of a beautiful raven haired woman whom he has never seen before, and who flings herself into his arms, sobbing and calling him Herbert.

Henry Cleaver thinks it is possible that he has been hypnotized or drugged, and that while in this condition his teeth have been extracted and his mouth used as a hiding place for the jeweled teeth by some desperate band of international crooks who have taken this method of getting the teeth from Washington to New York; but he still cannot understand how it was that he was able to make the journey from Washington to New York in seven minutes. It is some time before he gets the clue to this mystery.

Cleaver is taken to Washington and conducted to the offices of the Chief of the Secret Service. He is locked in and told to wait there until the Chief, who
is playing pinochle with the Secretary of the Treasury, can get time to talk with him.

CHAPTER ELEVEN

Cleaver waited for hours.

From the next room he could hear the merry laughter of the Cabinet officer and the detective chief as one or the other made a clever stroke.

But it did not cheer him.

Suddenly he heard a typewriter which stood near the Chief's desk begin to click. At first he thought it was working itself.

Then he saw that the machine was being operated by a gigantic cockroach.

He looked at what the beast was writing.

It began:

anything you say will
be used against you but you
must be careful and talk willingly and
without concealing anything
as silence will be
construed as a confession of guilt

i am warning you as a friend
do not act stiff and
offended but be careful and not try
to appear at your ease that awakens
suspicion act a little anxious
but try and not appear
nervous as that will make a bad
impression

But at that instant the door opened and the Secretary of the Treasury and the Chief of the Secret Service appeared with heavy shackles in their hands.

They flung Cleaver to the floor, handcuffed him, shackled his ankles, put him into a straitjacket, bound him to iron rings in the wall and gagged him, and then sat down and lighted their cigarettes.

"Where," said the Chief, proceeding to the examination, "is the body?"

"Sir," said the Secretary, "how dare you stand there with every evidence of a criminal nature showing in your attitude and demeanor and conceal from the authorities the reason for your arrest?"

(To be continued.)

archy del puerto rico

dear archy
thought you wd like a little letter
from your cousin in puerto rico
puerto rico is a hot country
we have lizards and politicians both
there are more of them than anything
except our family
wd you like to hear about them
well
yesterday i saw a track in the sand
three toes   three toes   three toes
      three toes   three toes
i followed the way the toes pointed
nothing there

i went back at the
other end of the track
a lizard was warming his
patent backbone
in the sun
in front of him sat
a gold fly fat like a buddha

lizard was gazing at fly
i was touched
i said to myself
the fly is his deity
he is saying his prayers to that fly
i will respect his devotions
suddenly
there was no fly
you don t have lizards in new york do
        you
well archy this is nice i am sure
so no more
from yr cousin

                    archy del puerto rico

hark

the ku klux klan
is going strong
and the national
emblem will soon be
the great
american kleagle

        archy

in a stew

i dropped into
a clam chowder the
other evening
for a warm bath and
a bite to eat
and i heard a couple of
clams talking
it seems that they

are sore on the
oyster family and
have formed an
organization to

do away with them
they call it the
ku klux klam
yours for the frequent stew

           archy

the burning question

BULLETIN: Maybe the Ku Klux Klams get
the information on which they act
from the Ouija Board

boss i can
throw some light
on the paragraph
above perhaps
as follows
said the scrammel to the weasel
as the kleagle wiggled by
there s the passion of a measle
in his sad and strangling cry
said the weasel to the scrammel
as the kleagle sang his note
there s the gurgle of a camel
in the gargle of his throat
said the werble to the wobble
as his larynx looped the loop
he burbles like a bobble
that is scalded eating soup
and they went and asked the ouija
the secret of his song
and it said his brain was squeegy
and his mind wasn t strong
yours for the higher
ministries of poesy

        archy

the thing to do

i went into a
barber shop the other
day where a lady
was having her little
girl s hair cut
and her husband was
getting shaved in the
next chair
in walked two
members of a patriotic
organization called the
krew krux kranks
with masks on and
carrying american flags
one of them seized a razor
and severed the
jugular vein of the
man in the chair who was
getting shaved saying
as he did so there now
mister bill billups i
reckon you will no longer
trouble the swiggles
of the insolvent empire
goodness gracious said the
lady that man
you have just sliced in two
at the neck was not
mister bill billups
at all i saw mister

bill billups getting off
a street car just five
minutes ago that man
you have just sliced in two
was mister pete perkins
and my husband
boo hoo hoo now i
am a widow
great guns said the
krew krux krank
lady i am as sorry as
sorry can be
but you must realize
that in our business we are
bound to make mistakes
sometimes he just looked like
mister bill billups lying there
in the chair all
lathered up
yes said the widow
it was a terrible mistake
but i can see that in your
line of work you are bound
to make mistakes
we are said the krew krux krank
but i cannot tell you
how bad i feel about this madam
you must not take it to heart
so much said the widow
anybody is likely
to make mistakes
but i do said the krew krux krank
i offer you a thousand
apologies i never
made a faux pas
like that before in all

my experience
oh well said the widow
do not take on so over it
i am sure that
it was quite unintentional
i look to the motive
behind it rather than
to the deed itself
but madam he began
do not be tiresome she
said interrupting him i quite
understand how it occurred
you are what i call
a sensible woman said the krew
krux krank
thank you said she
smiling and dimpling prettily
at the compliment come
little precious she said to her
child let us go home and see
if papa left any life
insurance policies around
anywhere
well said the krew krux krank
to the barber
i wish that everybody
would take the same
enlightened view of our
activities and realize
that in our great
patriotic work accidents
are bound to occur
it takes all sorts of people
to make a world
said the barber
which when you think of it

is just what a barber
always says about things
well boss this is one
tragic story with a cheerful
and happy ending
personally however i think
that the krew
krux kranks
should be prosecuted
under the law
which forbids using
the american flag
for trade purposes
there ought to be somebody
like the armenians in this
country the turks kill
the armenians and the
armenians are used to it
and nothing comes of it
but in this country people
who want to kill people
have no one like the armenians
to pick on
and trouble and unrest follow
their killings
why not have a million
people volunteer to be armenians
so the krew krux kranks
would not get into trouble
i do not pretend to be
a statesman but it is plain
to me that something should be
done about it that by
the way is what the barber said
also he looked in a puzzled
way at the remnants

of mister pete perkins
and he said i think
something should be done

archy

The

Great False Teeth

Mystery

Wedded and Parted

By the Author of The Great Goulash Mystery

Halleck Higglesworth is an Egyptologist of note. When he is not digging among the ruins of ancient Egypt he dwells alone in a mysterious house on Brooklyn Heights . . . alone, except for forty mummies, who have become more alive to him than are his breathing contemporaries.

He converses with these mummies and believes that they answer him. He sits for hours playing for them on the saxophone. He claims that at certain times they become reanimated by his personality or something and walk about with him.

He has a Ford car and frequently takes four or five mummies for a drive, setting them up stiffly in the car and talking to them as he drives through the streets.

These agreeable eccentricities lead to the belief among his neighbors that he is not quite sound mentally, a theory which Higglesworth himself bitterly repudiates. Persons from Manhattan who see him going about with his mummies do not notice anything strange, however; they only remark with that supercilious air so habitual with the Manhattanite: "How odd these old Brooklynites are!"

One evening, after Higglesworth has taken one of the Shepherd Kings to the theater with him, where they have occupied a box together, he gets the notion, as he is giving the King a drink and putting him into bed, that his Majesty has a guilty look upon his brown countenance. Higglesworth often notices these changes of expression in his mummies, although other persons cannot see them. Tightly clasped in the Shepherd King's hand is a set of remarkable false teeth, wrought of gold and platinum and ivory with gems scattered amongst them here and there.

His first thought is that the King has plucked them from

his own mouth, but a glance convinces the expert that these teeth are not of Egyptian manufacture. His second thought is that the King has stolen them from someone else at the theater.

While he is puzzling over the teeth he notices a gigantic cockroach crawl out of a sarcophagus and proceed to his typewriter, where the animal begins to write, butting the keys with his head.

CHAPTER TWELVE

The cockroach wrote laboriously.

Higglesworth drew nearer and read the following cryptic utterance:

> maybe the teeth that you have on
> once bit the dust at malplaquet
> your grandsires grandpas grandad john
> wore the same false teeth that you dis
>   play
> beautiful teeth they never turn gray
> dead are the men of the age of gold
> but their teeth are chewing rag today
> wonderful teeth they never grow old

somebody s selling or putting in pawn
teeth that were lost in the subsequent
    fray
when caesar hopped over the rubicon
to eat em alive on the appian way
beautiful teeth they never turn gray
the blooming bicuspids of hector the bold
are slicing spaghetti in yonder cafe
wonderful teeth they never grow old

the prehistorical mastodon
a pilocene chesterton nonchalant gay
how far have the mastodon s molars
    gone
since he recklessly laughed at the rocks
    in his hay
beautiful teeth they never turn gray
a thousand times they are bought and
    sold
man s teeth remain though his arts decay
wonderful teeth they never grow old

but dentist no seconds for me i say

Just at that instant the door was broken open and four
detectives entered. They flung Higglesworth aside and rush-
ing up to the Shepherd King, put him under arrest.

CHAPTER THIRTEEN

The mummy remained calm.

"darn it all," wrote the cockroach on the typewriter, "i am always interrupted by something before i can get a ballade finished."

CHAPTER FIFTEEN

The four detectives began a thorough survey of the Higglesworth house, arresting mummy after mummy.

Three patrol wagons stood outside, and the mummies were hustled into the wagons and driven to the nearest police station where charges of disorderly conduct were entered against them so that they could be legally held until the police found them guilty of something more important.

CHAPTER SIXTEEN

Archy, the Cockroach Detective, left alone in the mysterious house, began an examination of a thumb print which had rubbed off the teeth and fallen to the floor when the teeth were wrenched from the hand of the Shepherd King.

It was a dainty, feminine thumb print!

Here was a clue!

What could it lead to?

Archy knew!

(To be continued.)

please no rain

do you know of
any firm that specializes
in galoshes for cockroaches
it would be a
graceful deed if
you were to give me a
pair for my birthday
or a little motor boat
would do i

tried to get on the subway
train to go up town the
other day but a
cascade caught me on the
steps and carried
me onto the

tracks when i stopped
floating i was in
brooklyn

archy

a seaside spectacle

i saw a piece in the
paper not long ago where
you said the sea
serpent is no longer to be
seen i doubt if this is
strictly true i
was down by the water
front the other day and
overheard the
conversation of a couple of
gentlemen who had
just returned from a
visit to one of the
hooch ships out beyond the
twelve mile line they
had spent several days
on board and one of them
had seen the flying
dutchman scoot by in a
dead calm filled with
dodo birds and cubist posters
and the other one
said he missed that but he
had seen something
equally as good as he would have
called it a sea
serpent he said but that
it started to talk to
him it is my own
opinion that the

hooch boats are bringing
back the romance
to navigation
yours for the
amphibious life

          archy

archy declares neutrality

well boss there are
some great questions before us these
days such
as which shall i be a militarist or
a pacifist as between the two things i
am more or less neutral some days i
say on with the dance let war be
unconfined i
am a militarist other days i shout let
loose the dogs of peace and the
average i strike is one of complete
neutrality between the two last evening
after
you left some of the gang gathered
on your desk a couple of cockroaches
a red eyed
spider a mouse with a set of german
military
whiskers who is believed to be a
spy a big blue bottle fly that has been
asleep behind the radiator all winter
and we had
all decided on militarism when in blew a
hornet what is the question before the
house he
asked and when we told him he said if
this bunch is
for militarism count me a pacifist
or vice versa he said
anything for trouble i especially hate

spiders my grandfather got tangled up
in a web little red eye do you want
any of my
game i have not said a word remarked
the little red
eyed spider stranger go in peace you
hadn t better
say a word either said the hornet
i give you
warning that wherever i look i
create a barred zone i
will sink you without visit or search
stranger
said little red eye i never brag but
my bite
is poison where my tongue stabs a
life ceases if i was to spit on the floor a
poison flower would bloom there i
never boast myself
said the hornet i am a quiet person
but it is
only fair to tell you that i can lick my
weight in
german measles declare yourself
spider whatever you
are i am the other thing stranger said
the spider i
advise you to begin nothing that you are
not able to carry to a conclusion i feel
sorry for you stranger i hate to see an
innocent thing from the suburbs get
entangled with
a concentrated essence of pestilence like
myself come come said the hornet let
the note writing
cease i dare you dare me to do what asked
the spider dare

you to live any longer said the hornet
and they
went at it then the results were fatal
to both the
hornet stung the spider to death
and died of his own
wounds crying out for water to
the last watching
that fight made me more neutral
than ever if
possible

archy

The
Great False Teeth
Mystery
or
The Bolshevist's Bride

By the Author of The Great Goulash Mystery

Wilton Endicott, a young man of great wealth and studious tastes, falls in love with a haughty looking wax lady in the window of a department store, and vows he will never marry until he meets a living woman who is the counterpart in flesh and blood of the beautiful and aristocratic creature. He buys the figure from the department store and travels

about the world hunting for his ideal, devoting his ample leisure and great wealth to the research.

In one of the famous galleries of Italy he finds a portrait which is exactly like his ideal, and buys that also, carrying it with him.

The next year he finds on an island in the Grecian archipelago a marble statue, probably by Praxiteles, which is also exactly like the wax lady and exactly like the portrait. He purchases this also, and takes it with him in his hunt for the incarnate goddess.

Late in the year 1918 he finds embedded in one of the Alpine glaciers a woman in a perfect state of preservation who would be his ideal woman if she were only alive. The experts say that she has been in the ice 2,000 years, and was likely a Roman patrician. He buys her also, and keeps her in an especially constructed refrigerating room on board his private yacht—the name of which, by the way, is CHERCHEZ LA FEMME.

That same winter he gets a fleeting glimpse of his ideal woman on the screen at a movie show; but there is a fire in the theater and the film is burned and he can never find it again.

And then, early in 1919, he actually does find, in Siam, his goddess in the flesh.

But, unfortunately, there are two of her, just alike, and she is twins.

Still more unfortunately, she is Siamese twins.

Under the laws of Siam he could marry both twins. But Wilton Endicott is guided rather by morality than by the letter of the law, and he does not think this would be right.

He buys the twins, however, employing a chaperone for them, and takes them aboard his yacht, adding them to his collection, consisting of the wax lady, the portrait, the statue and the frozen girl.

He continues his search, hoping to find his ideal done up, so to speak, in a single package; his problem is to find the woman he saw on the movie screen.

If he cannot find this woman he feels he will die a disappointed man. Mentally considered, the twins are no great shakes; neither one of them is an intellectual giantess; the left hand twin is, in fact, feeble minded, and the right hand twin is becoming so rapidly through constant association with her sister.

Wilton Endicott is so saddened that he takes to writing poetry and also vers libre.

One day as he was in his study on his private yacht, engaged on a sonnet series entitled ELUSION, ILLUSION, AND DELUSION, a woman walks aboard the gangplank, enters his study, and lays on his desk a set of richly wrought false teeth made of ivory, gold and platinum, with gems scattered among them here and there.

It is his Ideal Woman.

CHAPTER NINETEEN

Wilton Endicott rose and was about to clasp her in his arms, with a glad cry.

His arms closed in on empty air.

There was no woman there!

She had vanished!

Had it been a dream?

It might well be.

But no!

Not an ordinary dream at least!

For the false teeth still lay on his desk. They were solid reality.

He ordered his crew to search every nook and cranny of the CHERCHEZ LA FEMME.

CHAPTER TWENTY

While they were engaged in this, the bo's'n piped himself aft and laid on Wilton's desk a neatly engraved card which read:

BAXTER SMITHERS, JR.
PSYCHIC EXPERT
MATERIALIZATIONS A SPECIALTY
SATISFACTION GUARANTEED

"Usher him in," said Wilton.

The bo's'n piped Baxter Smithers, Jr. aft.

"The psychical research society to which I belong," said Mr. Smithers, "is looking for a Spirit. A Spirit whom we call Elinora. We succeeded in materializing Elinora last year. Unfortunately her fad for being materialized has so grown upon her that latterly she has refused to be unmaterialized again except of her own volition. She wanders about and gives us no end of trouble.

"She is likely," said Mr. Smithers, "to pop up anywhere at any time. She gets our little group in bad. Especially since she takes things. Elinora isn't honest, I regret to say" —

"You lie!" cried Wilton Endicott, and sprang at his throat.

76

He would have killed Baxter Smithers then and there if he had not reflected that without the psychic expert's assistance he might never become better acquainted with Elinora.

"Excuse me," he said, "for my impetuosity—but I love Elinora. I have sworn that she shall be my bride."

"Too bad, too bad," said Baxter Smithers. "Don't you know Elinora is already married?"

"Gawd!" moaned Wilton Endicott and fell senseless upon the rich Oriental rug.

The bo's'n ran in, and seeing the situation piped the butler aft with a glass of brandy.

Baxter Smithers fancied that the teeth moved as the brandy came into the cabin, as if a ghostly tongue had clicked against them.

But this may have been only fancy.

Psychic experts are apt to imagine such things.

It was cognac.

CHAPTER TWENTY-ONE

The aroma pervaded the room.

Those present could scarcely think of anything else.

Suddenly Elinora materialized and grasped the glass. She drank, too.

The Siamese twins ran in at this instant.

The door of the refrigerating room burst open and the frozen lady was propelled into the room by an unseen force.

Wilton Endicott opened his eyes and saw the four women exactly alike, weeping and glaring at each other. "Gawd!" said Wilton, and fainted once more.

He was not happy.

The good ship CHERCHEZ LA FEMME sailed on into the unknown.

(To be continued.)

archy interjects

what right do you
have to put me into
that fiction story
you are writing without obtaining
my formal consent
or giving me extra
pay take me
out of that great false
teeth mystery at once
or else double my
salary

                    archy

archy afloat

wireless to the sun dial
u s s oriziba dec 2 all at sea
well boss here am i
your own archy
i stowed away in
a steamer
trunk and shall
report i
have already found several
relatives and ship
mates of former years on
board the vessel the
grub is probably better
in some spots on this
ship than in others but
so far i have only
struck the others

archy

archy to the radio fans

. .

— — . . — . .. —

— . — — — — — .. —

.... — — — . — —

.. ....

— . — — — — — .. — . — .

. — — . — ... — .

. — .. . — . — — . — ....

— — — — — .. . — — . — —

archy

tossing with a porpoise

london england
november the eighth
by wireless
to home
boss i have
had a series of the most
terrible and nerve sapping
adventures since
i last saw you
i got onto the little
paquebot to cross the
channel and half way
over to dover it began
to stand on its ear
i noticed
that the boat had a
cauliflower ear
i think it stands on
its larboard ear habitually
i suddenly found myself
propelled through the air
and for my sins
i alighted in the lap
of an english lady
who called me a nawsty bug
and tossed me
into the restless deep
as casually as you would
blow the foam from a glass
of beer if you

could get a glass of
beer in that god s country
in which you live
all seemed lost
including life
and luncheon
but by the grace of providence
i fell upon the fat wet back

of a porpoise
who finally landed me
in the thames
i am now living
in westminster abbey

if you want to call
my present existence
living i wish you
would at once
start something calculated
to get me back
to america
i feel depressed here
and there is too much
competition for any one
to be able to
make a living in london
by being depressed

archy

back with a message

well boss here i am
back from
my trip abroad
and with lots
of adventures
to relate but i
refuse to
tell any of them
unless you give
me a raise
i will
have to be raised
from nonpareil type
to brevier
minion will not
do if you consent
let me know by
printing this in
brevier

archy

The

Great False Teeth

Mystery

or

Broken Vows

By the Author of The Great Goulash Mystery

Wentworth Chisholm has seven beautiful daughters, three of whom have blue eyes and three of whom have brown eyes. The seventh daughter, more beautiful than any of the others, has one blue eye and one brown eye, which gives her an effect of piquancy and strangeness quite irresistible to all her suitors. The seven daughters conduct a manicuring establishment in New York City, and might become wealthy beyond the dreams of avarice were it not for the extravagant generosity of Wentworth Chisholm himself.

Sane on all other subjects, he has the hallucination that he is Santa Claus and that every night is Christmas Eve. He wears a long white flowing beard, and his costume is the

familiar conventional one of St. Nicholas. Night after night he goes out upon the roofs with packets of presents which he has purchased from his daughters' earnings—and they, devoted children that they are, can deny him nothing—and attempts to crawl down chimneys. Most chimneys are too small for him; and he is continually getting stuck in chimneys; he is frequently burned and occasionally almost suffocated.

After he has tried for some hours to get down a chimney he usually gives it up and flings his presents down the chimney anyhow, or gives them to people in the streets.

It is necessary, for his protection, that he be followed. One of the daughters devotes herself to him one night, and another the next night.

The girl with the different eyes is named Thyrza, but she is nicknamed Thursday, as that is her night to look after her father; her sister Freda is nicknamed Friday; Mona is called Monday, Tessie is Tuesday, and so forth.

One Thursday evening, after old Chisholm has given away his last package to a man who has helped Thyrza pluck him from a chimney, the man draws from his coat pocket a little box and says:

"I will accept your present, sir, if you will take this in return."

Wentworth Chisholm refuses.

CHAPTER TWENTY-THREE

"But I will take your gift," said Thursday, smiling, for she saw that the stranger had fallen in love with her, and felt strangely drawn to him. She stepped from the shadow of the chimney into the bright moonlight and opened the box.

It contained a set of false teeth made of gold and platinum and ivory, with rare gems among them here and there.

And sitting beside the teeth was a large cockroach.

"What an extraordinary present," she said. "My sisters and I have received many presents from our customers—indeed, if we did not accept them, father's little amusements would quite ruin us financially—but this . . . "

She turned toward the stranger.

He was gone.

At that instant four detectives leapt upon the roof and leveled automatic pistols at her head.

"Ha! Madame Z!" cried the leader of the band. "Trapped at last! And with the teeth in your possession! You had best come with us without any trouble!"

Thursday appealed to her father, but the old gentleman was presenting the other three detectives with his watch and chain, his seal ring and his gold rimmed glasses, smiling delightedly upon these new friends.

Thursday realized that her father was but a broken reed to lean upon.

CHAPTER TWENTY-FOUR

Doctor after doctor had examined him.

But no physician had been able to say just what the matter was.

All agreed, however, that it was something mental.

Thursday rapidly reflected that in the present emergency there was not time to consult another physician.

She must trust her own wits.

"Sir," she said to the chief of the detective band, "is this Madame Z of whom you speak blue-eyed or brown-eyed?"

If he said blue-eyed the clever minx intended to show him her brown eye and thus escape.

Or vice versa.

The detective consulted a memorandum book.

"One eye," he said, "is blue, and one eye is brown."

Thursday fainted and was taken unconscious to the

police station, where she was shackled and flung into a cell.

When she awakened from her swoon the cockroach was making signs at her

What could the insect be up to?

We shall see.

(To be continued.)

waxing poetic

come fill the cup
for spring is here
be frivolous
come on
and sup on cheese
and beer
don t drivel us with
moral talk and guff about
eternity o

do not squawk so rough
about modernity my gosh
it s spring the
world is young and
free again a little fling
is being flung
by me again
dangerous change of meter slow down

april s full of showers may s
a month of moons nothing
known in flowers can
compare with joon s
nothing known approached paradise
like spring that is why
the roaches
slap their chests
and sing
i mean to say
i m exhilirated
beyond words i found
a bit of chartroose on
the desk
just now

                           archy

thanks boss

thank you boss
for putting me into
brevier type
instead of nonpareil
or minion
i regard it as
a raise in salary
and will work on in
contentment henceforth
and say nothing
about food or
clothing this winter
i will get through somehow
as i have got through
other winters
you certainly know how
to appeal to the
vanity of the artist
your faithful little
bug

                archy

archy gets historical

this lenin person
seems to be the
most active hero in
captivity in the course
of one week he has
been bombed poisoned
and become insane he has resigned
died a natural
death confessed
everything denied all
given up in despair
and planned
four new offensives
i will say he is
active i
never knew of but
one more active creature
that was a chameleon
with whom i was
acquainted i
met him one day looking
rather fatigued and
pale not to say
washed out well joe
i said to him for his
name was joe
you look a little peaked
today what is the
chief trouble archy he
said i am worn out i

admit it i have been
too active lately
a week ago i fell into
a kaleidoscope
belonging to a seven year old
kid and i coundn t get
out it was a favorite
toy of that child s and
he has been looking into
it and turning it ever
since for one whole
week archy i
have been what you
might call active but
i have been faithful to my
duty i have kept up
with that kaleidoscope
color for color and change
for change it has made
a nervous wreck of me but
i have not shirked my
duty this morning
thank god the thing was stepped
on and broken and i
made my escape
it strikes me that
lenin will wear himself
out like that
chameleon if he is
too ambitious he ought to
rest up for a week
stick to carbuncles or
some one thing for a while
and take it easy

                         archy

archy remembers

well boss i had a
terrible adventure the
other day it was the
day that the news
of the armistice came which
afterward proved not to be
true if you can
remember that far
back
i was on one of the upper
floors of the
woolworth building and as
you may have noticed it has many
upper floors and some of the
uppermost floors are
very far up
this floor was about six
hundred feet above
broadway
i was hunting bits of
sandwich in a waste
paper basket when the
paper shower began
everybody began to
hunt paper to tear up and
throw out the window and to
make a frightful story as
mild as possible i
was on one of the pieces of
paper that was torn and

thrown out of the
window down down down
i went whirling around and around
for a hundred feet and
screaming at the
top of my voice but in
all that noise what were the
cries of one small cockroach
i doubt if i was heard
twenty feet away
down and down i fell and just as i
thought i might be dashed to pieces on
some bald head two hundred yards
    below
a gust of wind caught me and up up
    up

i went again to make
a tall story as short as
possible this kept up for
nearly two hours i
felt like a person who
has climbed aboard an
airplane thinking it is
an automobile and who
does not discover his
mistake until he
is above some brutal looking
mountain range
i finally came into contact with a
piece of ticker tape
and crawled aboard it in
midair it seemed bigger somehow
but it evidently
thought it was a snake it
went wreathing and twining
itself through the air
and when it finally did come
down it twined itself around the
neck of an inebriated
gentleman who saw me and
whose first words were
i do not see a cockroach i
only think i see a cockroach
o heaven if i only
get over this attack i
will never drink another
drop yours as ever

                    archy

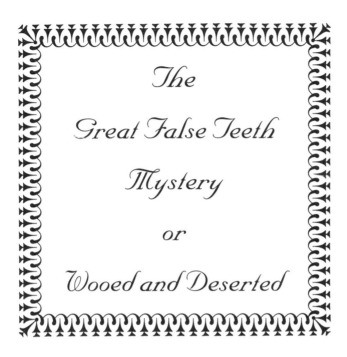

The

Great False Teeth

Mystery

or

Wooed and Deserted

By the Author of The Great Goulash Mystery

"be careful," wrote Archy, the Cockroach Detective, on the typewriter, "and do not put those teeth into your mouth and chew with them on anything very hard or unyielding, and do not drop them."

"Why not?" asked the Inspector from Scotland Yard.

"they are loaded," wrote Archy.

"Loaded?"

"those teeth were presented eight years ago to the late czar of russia," explained Archy, "by an anarchist who wanted to get rid of him, and who disguised himself as a politician and became a cabinet minister in order to win the czar s confidence.

"they are very old, thousands of years old, and of great historical value besides their intrinsic value. it was this that made them a present worthy of offering to the czar. he was delighted at the prospect of owning them.

"but the last molar on the lower right hand side the anarchist hollowed out, and in the cavity he placed a charge of high explosive capable not only of blowing the czar s head off, but of wrecking the palace. then he sealed the cavity and gave the teeth to the czar.

"the czar often used them, wearing them haughtily at state banquets, and when smiling at his people from the imperial automobile, in his progress through the streets of st petersburg, now petrograd.

"the anarchist, who posed as a cabinet member, used to sit at the state banquets waiting for the teeth to explode, but they never did.

"the reason was that for several years prior to his death the czar was afflicted with a nervous disease, and his physicians restricted him to a diet of broths and gruels. he never really chewed on the loaded teeth.

"then came the war, and later the revolution. when the czar s palace was looted by the reds, the teeth were taken. there was little to eat in russia, and the teeth were smuggled out of the country and sold.

"but the charge of high explosive still remains in the last molar on the lower right hand side; they are still exceedingly dangerous."

"Dear me!" said the Scotland Yard man, moving away from the vicinity of the teeth.

Archy picked them up and started out of the room with them, crawling along the ceiling and walls, toward the open window which gave on to the fire escape.

"But, I say!" cried the Scotland Yard man. "Cockroach! You are making away with those teeth, you know! Bring them back!"

Archy's only reply was to dangle the teeth loosely from his forelegs, indicating that if he were pursued or interfered with he would drop them and everything in the vicinity would be destroyed. The Scotland Yard man got the point.

Archy crawled out onto the fire escape. The Scotland Yard man followed, but at a safe distance. He knew that the cockroach, if he were interfered with, would drop the teeth to the pavement fifty feet below and destroy the building in which they stood.

He ceased to follow.

Archy chuckled.

He had the teeth.

And they were not really loaded at all.

(To be continued.)

archy saves the fleet

well boss after a series of
adventures more thrilling than anything
that ever happened to
sindbad the sailor i
found myself clinging to
the top of a german
periscope 800 miles off the
coast of new england any moment the

vessel might submerge and
it would take me hours to wade ashore
    suddenly
i saw a fleet of

vessels coming in our direction heavens
    it
was a flock of ships carrying american
soldiers and supplies to france had the
submarine seen it yet i asked
myself i must save that covey
of transports at all costs in a
moment my plan was laid i climbed
onto the lens of the periscope and began
to run rapidly back and forth across
    it with an
undulating movement as if
i were a ship presently i heard a voice
    in german
floating up the tube of the periscope
    which i
translate for the
convenience of your readers heinie said
    the
voice look out the periscope and see if
any transports are about high high
your ayeness i mean aye aye your high
    ness said
heinie and a moment later he
exclaimed i see a queer ship
shaped like a cockroach skooting over
    the
waters of the atlantic fool let me look
    you
have been inhaling too much oil said the
commanding officer i redoubled my
efforts to look like a ship it is too true
    said
the commanding officer the americans
have launched some
terrible new invention in the foreground
is a

vessel like a cockroach and behind it is
a fleet i can scarcely make out but
likely they are all composed of these
new hellish inventions what fiendish
practices they put into operation
against us
poor innocent submariners let us
sink at once and do it as
spurlos as possible an instant later the
vessel had sunk and i was on my way
to the
bevy of american ships i had
just saved

                                        archy

eating for art s sake

well boss we may
be legally at war but
i am derned if i can
make myself feel like it was war
time wait says mehitabel the
cat till the food shortage comes then
you will know it is war

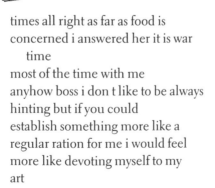

times all right as far as food is
concerned i answered her it is war
   time
most of the time with me
anyhow boss i don t like to be always
hinting but if you could
establish something more like a
regular ration for me i would feel
more like devoting myself to my
art

                          archy

The

Great False Teeth

Mystery

CHAPTER THIRTY CONCLUDED

"So then," said the Duchess, "there is no other way but this!"

And before anyone could prevent her she swallowed the teeth, and an instant later that stormy and beautiful spirit had passed beyond the cares and misunderstandings and disillusionments of this world.

"Sonia!" cried Harold Hefflefinger. "Why didst thou not save some of those teeth for me? I would fain have perished with thee!"

But Sonia, for obvious reasons, did not answer.

"Then that is the end . . . the end?" murmured Harold Hefflefinger.

"it is the end," said the Detective.

And it was . . . the end . . . the end . . .

(THE END)

archy still treats em rough

archy
i once read
of a painting
where a woman is depicted
pulling out her heart
to hand it to a man
and he takes it

but scorns her
and the joke is
that when one heart
comes out
another one
grows in its place

and so she is kept busy
giving away
what is not appreciated
and all i have to remark
is that on account
of your rude letter
my enthusiasm for you
has been dampened
why i don t even know
what you look like
and if i did see you
even though you are
so smart
after one look i would most probably
have run away

                    jennie the cockroach

        p s archy
        a month ago
        i wrote you
        two poems
        and i am still waiting
        to find out
        what happened

When the above letter was shown to Archy he dictated the
following reply:

        tell her the
        best time
        to run away
        is before she takes
        the first look
        i don t want
        any of her hearts
        they sound too

frequent to me
p s ate
the poems

archy

meter reading

autumn is here
and the dactyl
droops its weary wing
  and the sad iambic
    shivers
      with frozen feet
        poor thing
          but spring will come
            and the poets
              will thaw
              and the fountains gush
              and a hundred
              million dactyls
              twitter
                amid the slush

archy

sport to you

in constantinople
it has been
a favorite sport
to take poor little
cockroaches and make
them race till
they fell exhausted
when i first heard of it
i said these turks

are not the right
sort of people
and events
have shown i was
right

                    archy

archy says

one advantage
of being a cockroach
is that i see
things from the under
side

* * *

some of these
egyptian styles
make a great hit with
me any girl
that wears them
ought to be able to
go right out and
win a mummy

* * *

one ghost that
sir arthur conan
doyle has never yet
got into
communication with
so far as he has
ever reported is the
ghost of edgar
allen poe the author of
the murders in the rue
morgue and other

stories applying the
detective method
to the detection of
crime

* * *

i do not
notice
hungarian goulash

in the restaurants
any more
but irish stew
is equally
as good

* * *

the dachsund
thinks the giraffe

is a very
queer looking
animal

archy

a final thought

i could tell you what
poetry is but
why should i stir up
feelings yours for
vers d archibald

archy

t h e   e n d